Near
the
Fire

Near
the
Fire

Poems by

PHILIP K. JASON

 DRYAD PRESS

Washington, DC & San Francisco

103700

Acknowledgements
The author wishes to thank the editors and publishers of the following periodicals in whose
pages many of these poems first appeared. *Agni Review*: "Florida: December 1964";
Centennial Review: "Bedtime Story" and "The Old Place"; *Chesapeake Country Life*:
"Crossing the Chesapeake in Winter"; *Cimarron Review*: "Lines on Lines";
Commonweal: "Definition" and "Heat Wave"; *Dryad* "Spacebound" and "Waitress";
Four Quarters: "Suppose They Came Unbuttoned"; *Kansas Quarterly*: "Getting to Me,
Getting to You"; *Midstream*: "Caesaria" and "At the Lebanese Border"; *Outerbridge*:
"Farm Auction: Accident, Maryland"; *Phoebe*: "Too Long"; *Poem*: "Body Language";
Poetry Now: "The Women Who Feared Statues"; *Remington Review*: "Homage to Luis
Tiant"; *Southern Poetry Review*: "Sometimes, Late in the Night"; *Webster Review*: "Bus
Number One," "The Price of Survival," "The Dead Sea," "Change," and "The Red
Sea"; *West Coast Poetry Review*: "My Fifties Girl"; *Wind*: "Recitation."

"Morning in Mill Valley" and " My Fifties Girl" also appear in the chapbook *Thawing
Out* (Dryad Press, 1979).

"Once You Know How" first appeared in the anthology *The Ear's Chamber* (SCOP
Publications, 1981).

This publication has been partially supported by grants from the National Endowment
for the Arts, a Federal agency and the Maryland Arts Council

Library of Congress Cataloging in Publication Data

Jason, Philip K., 1941-
    Near the fire.
    I.Title.
PS3560.A66N4 1983   811'.54   83-1488
ISBN 0-931848-56-3
ISBN 0-931848-55-5 (pbk.)

Published by
DRYAD PRESS

15 Sherman Avenue
Takoma Park, Maryland 20912

P.O. Box 29161 Presidio
San Francisco, California 94123

To Ruth
with love

Contents

III

IV

I

Meeting the Day

His hands are fish that dart
to the center of ripples
at the surface of his name;
his neck is a knotted trunk
that shoots from a mulch of collar;
his arteries surge with coffee.
He moves to the garbage truck's moan
and counts out busfare in his pocket's dark.
Today, he is going to be on time.
He pulls on his tie
and his eyes become paired skaters
that veer through the red creases of dawn.

My Fifties Girl

My fifties girl,
when she ran to embrace me
behind the bleacher seats,
well, she really ran, fast,
and her waved hair flounced
like a yo-yo. Her gum-soled
oxfords sprung over pop caps
and we held each other real hard.

In the halls, by heel-bruised lockers,
we'd brush by careful chance;
the faint crackle of static,
her linty orlon sweater to my
starched pink shirt, that was thrill
enough for the rest of the day.

And in our risky secret places,
when we held each other's breath
forever while I undid whatever
couldn't be pulled away,
wishing the radio was on,
something like revelation
was gathering light to our eyes.

And to show you how long ago
this was, how truly the times change,
it seems now that we somehow pretended
a violent awe about the stitching
on her bra, some mystery of lace,
some holy woven grail to be won
from the close encumbrance of her breasts.

Versions of Fear

Sometimes I remember the energy fear,
not the fear of hurt or doubt,
but the one of sharp exhilaration.
I remember the late-night rides on the El,
thinly-peopled, to my stop in mid-Bronx,
and — one time — the aging, wine-soaked queer
who wagged his desperate smile in my face,
telling me how I dressed all wrong,
how I held my body clumsily,
and how, of course, he could show me . . .

And now at our staid, suburban parties
we tell — again, again— of our lives
in the knifeblade city, coursing with threat,
and go back to those life-giving days of fear:
my wife, her eyes dancing under the backyard stars,
tells of the handbag ripped from her grasp,
her frozen scream crossing to Astor Place
while the evening walkers watched their shoes;
I tell of my pickpockets, my winter hungers
brought on by the ravages of youth,
and, again, of the dumpy, balding queer
— out from behind a late-closing deli counter —
and our skirmish over his hand on my thigh.

I look out through the wide glass patio door
to the sweep of well-fed, uniformed shrubs,
and I see our track-jiggled heads reflect
in the stained windows of the subway car,
and, out of the corner of my eye,
the Puerto Rican dude in the far seat
mimes silent guffaws at these two fools:
the sodden, shrunken suitor
and his callow, angry, cool-keeping prey.

I can think of this now
as I sit in a solid, cavernous house,
my brand-name manhood intact,
attuned to the relative safety of distance,
regular hours, — all my heaped-up winnings.
There still can be threats; fights
can break out in this family
about which bank to keep our money in
or whether to spend some time
at the mountains or the shore.

Down from the El I'd glide,
hand on the pipe in my overcoat pocket,
never more wakeful, alive,
than when crossing before the seedy bar
and threading between the strewn drunks,
or staring down the part-time muggers and rollers,
thrilled to escape the dealers, pimps, and whores
who knew, somehow, that I was immune.

Or did they? Was I?
All of my safe and sane passages
have led me here to instant breakfasts,
to Merrill Lynch money managers,
to whimpering over the broken starter cord
on my adjustable mulching mower.
Perhaps it is right here, right now,
that I have been shot-up, overdosed,
mugged by everything I've gathered,
raped by everything I've fathered.
And *this* fear does not spark me
but bends me down to the sleep
from which I wake exhausted, sweaty,
something sharp beneath my ribs.

Sometimes I want to be out there again,
walking along the hard, bottom line
without this laving experience, this net.
I want to feel that everything's at stake
and there is no recourse.
I want to believe in the finality of words
like "hand it over kid" or "get lost"
or "are you ready for a little action?"
I want to look back into the sad eyes
of that little, smiling man
with purple splotches on his waiter's smock,
that man who disgusted me, whom I chased off,
who gave me a time that still,
after more than twenty years,
shines like the glistening skin
of any newborn thing.

Getting To Me, Getting To You

I'm tired of my world's geometry,
the way the sun is strained
through back alleys, loading docks,
and finally the paneled window
and the loosely woven curtains.
When it gets here
it's worn out, rubbed out.
So with the moon,
so with the sound of storm.

It seems, when a breeze
staggers to my cheek,
it's been honed, whittled,
reduced to begging
for acknowledgment.

Everything wild
reaches me second-hand,
filtered through what we have made.
Not only subdued, but framed.

And me? Is there a wildness
reaching out, disciplined
by halls and parking lots?
Is the shape I take
as you perceive me
a forfeit, too neatly shaven?

My nerves explode, you know,
like the heaving sun.

The Old Place

Other people's dogs are barking
in these now unvacant lots.
All the good spots
for Kool-Aid stands are striped for parking.

Trees planted in your youth
are stooping giants now; they have outraced
your own alarming pace.
The house is hidden by them, and the path

you wore between them now is lost
in the ungrassed shadows of their leaves.
Something you haven't found here grieves
for its absence: the last and least

of you that warred against these hedges,
bore scars from this daily battle,
and also from the fallen bottle
in which you drowned the captive beetles.

To this day you carry signs
of what you were in this old place,
but there is nothing of you here, no trace
of what you knew you wouldn't find.

The places you put on
don't cover you, the streets
don't press back to your feet,
no forest rears itself from this neat lawn.

Bedtime Story

Something small and dark lay crouched
at the back of my throat
waiting its slow souring wait
until it would wait no longer.

The boy was already cowering;
the words he'd said had dropped
like a heavy, poisonous dram
swirling the waters of our anxious love.

Who can tell why this needed
to be said, or why the closed bolt
of my rage could not hold tight against it?

It was the same old thing,
me calling him out for the forming man
in him filling the child's mouth with words.

Don't talk back to your father, I said.

But the spell would not be cast this time.
That man possessed the quavering child
and only the pale child's shell
stood before me. A voice like my own
unleashed a black hail against the trigger
of my resolve.

                And that dark thing
knew that its time had come again,
wheeled on fierce wings and grew
immense as the winter night.

I'd had to let go to gain myself back,
but the boy had no defense against it:
he could neither run nor strike it down,
only let it do its horror and spend itself
as all the demons finally do that spring from us,
unwanted, changing the colors of our hearts.

The Sideways Kiss

There is still your youth
that comes back in the sideways kiss
we make to get our
noses out of the way,
and there is still my youth
running along your back
with these two hands.

Your eyes are the same eyes
but looking into them now
it's harder to find you looking back:
down that deep well of children, debts, and doubts
is the dull flicker of a young wife's dream.

Our faces turn about
on the axis of our mouths
in a slow spin like the turning of a key
in a lock whose works have fallen out.

Our lashes brush, and our lips,
which almost form words as we kiss,
don't know the decade anymore
that we are meeting in

or why it takes such sorrow
to bring us back again
to the slow cycle of moments
in this closely shared life
and momentarily shared skin.

Messages

The stars transmit their messages
on strings of frost;
their meanings sit like pale dust
on our shoulders.
We turn toward each other's shadows
and our thoughts
collect like practiced signatures
upon the sheets.
Your dust and mine we mingle
in a hollow
of the night, in a cramped space,
generating back
the glow of our decypherings.
The stars turn too;
they do not see us watching.
They are in love
and do not care who knows it.
They wonder if
they are receiving messages
on threads of fire
from distant bodies burning out.

Sleeping Near The Fire

She is reading sleazy romances
whose covers show long-gowned virgins
racing away from glowering, one-eyed
castles. The moon is stuck next to
the price. The black-cloaked villain
glares out from a scraggy tree.
Below the border is a haven,
a handsome righter of her life,
perhaps a sparkling kitchen,
a trip to the hairdresser . . .
but for now all is lost.

She ends a chapter, turns to the man
sleeping his frivolous, selfish sleep.
And now she is ready to scream
at his deadness, his lack of romance,
his worrying over getting up on time,
and the cheap cracks about her
entertainments. She has grabbed all
the covers up around her.

He slowly awakes to the cold,
but nothing is said between them.
Only her subtle shivering pleads,
"Take me away from all this;
I'm yours, if you'll only warm me,
rub me with danger and care,
arrive in the final chapter
or be revealed no cold detainer
at last, but the true heir,
the mind whose clouds I've lifted
by my hot devotion, my unswerving

presence, my own warmth that will
burnish your noble soul
to the kind of lust that warms
me back again, that keeps me
pure with the flame of flesh,
each of us sleeping near the fire.''

Item: Man Injured By Flying Stump

. . . was critically injured yesterday when
a tree stump he was pulling from his yard
with his station wagon suddenly came free,
flew through the vehicle's rear window and
hit him in the back of the head.

For years the neighbors complained
about how he'd reduced the blighted tree
to a stump that blighted the whole block,
and then had left it there — a veteran
showing off its amputations.
These were good people who watered and mulched
and pruned; they hadn't earned this guilt
by association.
                        So one day his daughter
came home from school wet-eyed
from taunts and his holdout was done.
This was not a free country.
You couldn't parade your sawed-off stumps
on this field of good green taste.
From deep in the garage he pulled out
remnants of clothesline and blind-cord,
biting down hard on his dead cigar.
He scraped his knuckles to meat
lashing that stump to the wagon bumper
only to hear the whipsnap of failure
at the dumb lurch of low gear.

And he could tell the neighbors
were watching, doing compulsory headshakes.
Enraged, he brimmed with the big idea
of his rights, but his jaw got set
in the wrong position and his words
were like ground gears in his voicebox.

So he rented lengths of the nastiest chain,
hacked at roots, altogether bound himself
to the task that conferred defeat.
First the car gave a long grunt,
the taut chain catching the sun's snicker.
Then the mandrake shriek of the stump
and the man's head wobbling and pinging inside
like a spent lightbulb dandled between two fingers.

II

Spacebound

Space is tricky
stays right with me
cold   benign

me in the middle
carrying space around
in all directions.

Space is foxy
knows I'm waiting
to shake it off
to rub it off
with one quick turn.

Space pretends
we are silent friends
that everything is fine
between us
            and
between us.

Space will kill me
quicker than time.

Florida — December 1964

I remember the first
state-eating burst
of sixteen hours:
D.C. to Jacksonville,
the sudden showers
that fouled our camping gear
lashed to the trunk (the grill
stowed *inside* gave us planning qualms,
as did the over-loaded rear).
Our twenty roastbeef sandwiches were rare;
we chewed past elms and evergreens to palms,
only stopping to gas and piss.
Dead-tired, we took the first motel
and left our wives to sleep after one kiss.

Then we slowed down . . . the bikes and bells
of St. Augustine . . . Daytona . . . Lauderdale
(out of season — cheap). Malingerers
along the ocean coast, we camped in a gale,
unnerved by stories of the coral snake
that bites the web of flesh between your fingers,
the rain drumming on our tents, mostly awake
that night. Then to the subdivided beaches
of Miami, and off to skirt the sprinkled Keys,
and scratch through the Everglades, whose reaches
awed us: mangrove and rainbow birds. The pleas
of the girls annoyed us; the spanking pink
marina seemed to ruin the budget.

Next, up the gulf coast, that stainless sink
of jeweled villages that old folks covet,
and inland . . . Orlando . . . water skiers
(you scraped the bumper sticker off, got leers).

28

At last, weary and gritty, two-weeks tan,
we stumbled north onto the long streak back.
We bought a final sack of oranges, assorted jams
for gifts, ate half of them, wiggled up the track.
That was the best of all our holidays:
the key-lime pie, the fetid clothes for pillows,
red neon snapper signs, the endless highways
strewn with armadillos.

Waitress

After she brought the menus
she shrank, smiling, for the water,
then back, sudden, would we like to order
drinks first? Needing this excuse,

we took it: Scotch and soda.
We waited, this time, a little longer.
Pad under chin, she mixed the liquor
as if she had some quota

of trips to make and this
was called mix and write meal.
Hungry, we jumped to her appeal
and rattled off our list.

She stopped us. Arrogant?
No, nor servile. She made it clear
she was the pro. Time was *our* fear;
her hurry was efficient.

Now she led the antiphonal chant
of the entree number, rare or done;
potatoes, baked or fries; one
green vegetable (the sauce is bland);

Roquefort, Bleu, or French;
and what to drink. Our recitations
came on cue. There were no omissions
when she served. The wench!

Farm Auction: Accident, Maryland

This town grows widows faster than
Irwin Howard can auction a farm,
and he's the best.
Hear him play that crowd:
five tractors, three plows,
and a hay baler in a half hour.
Carl kept them almost like new.

The Enlows been here twenty-five years,
but the boys don't want it no more.
They tried, for Edna's sake, but they fell
to squabbling over who owned what
and who'd do what
and then they figured that they weren't
fighting over anything worth having,
just to scratch out something from dirt.

Now Irwin's people do it right.
This crowd is living it up,
and the food is even better
than at the Fire Department picnic.
He's just taken the whole thing
off Edna's hands.

> *Edna's hands* smooth a worn apron
> flat against her thighs. Nothing
> is going to change, she says to
> herself—I'll carry it all with me.
> The July sun floods through the trees
> in shafts. Irwin is holding an old oak rocker
> over his head. Caps flutter, hands wave
> in the air. "Sold." Edna tightens
> her fingers and follows the line of light
> to the end of a shelf of mason jars sealed and stacked.
> The widows huddle and whisper. One of her sons
> catches her elbow and hurries her into the shade.

Look at the out-of-towners.
They're going for crocks and old tools;
probably going to put them on curio shelves.
Probably going to get tired of them after a while
and put them out for sale in consignment shops.
Some of them even came to the picnic.
You should have seen them stomping their feet
to the fiddles, walking in wide circles
around the horseshit.

And Glotfelty's here,
scooping up handfuls of bridles and stirrups,
and handing them over to Irwin,
and then bidding up to three dollars a bunch.
Look at the widows watch him.
They can see themselves settling down
at that riding stable of his.
Glotfelty gets what he wants, though.
He don't need nothing from them.

What Irwin's got now
don't even belong to the Enlows.
They're just throwing everything in.
I remember just after Ben Small died,
his wife had Irwin sell off their place,
and one of those double-knit tourists
just out and reneged on his bid,
and Lizzy was stuck for a buggy.
That's it right there.
I guess Irwin figured he owed her.

> *He owed her*, thought Edna.
> He owed her for thirty-five years:
> the ten in Illinois, and then the hard move
> away from her family and down to this
> rough tag of Maryland. He owed her for
> seven children, hearty and full of life.
> Through the rat-a-tat-tat of Irwin's voice
> she could hear Carl muttering, fixing a combine

and then she felt herself down on the ground
in the cool milkhouse but no
she was out there next to her white farmhouse
the sun still blazing but tilting now
and Irwin holding up the headboard.
He was selling the bedroom set piece by piece.

And then Edna took her place in the huddle of widows,
the barn-red paint of her husband's death still fresh.

Bent Figures

Like beasts whose instincts shape their lives,
they migrate south and west to the great deserts
where they build their own mirages.
Many live alone, survivors of matings
whose grown offspring are strung out
along a map of telephone wires.
Their grounds, covered with pastel stones
and desert borrowings, look prehistoric;
here and there, a desolate birdbath
catches the sun. The sun is what
they've come here for, and the dryness
that pulls moisture from the skin.

Each is as bleached and tanned and stiff
as a bent figure in a crude museum
where skulls of animals that couldn't thrive
are found beneath the arms of saguaros.
What led them here? Gayly adorned,
their polished stones set
in the style of another culture,
these wizened gauchos
who gave us our eastern accents
ride herd on themselves now.

They call it living: not giving up,
taking free classes at the junior college,
defying arthritis with arts and crafts.
They hold the hands of strangers
and play at musical chairs
until none can hear the music
or when it stops:
first the brasses fade,
then the guitars,
then the single hissing maraca
gives back its sand.

Morning In Mill Valley

Mount Tamalpais is the Sleeping Princess,
her soft slopes prowled
by a serpent of fog.

Like a drugged coquette, sleep-teasing,
she passes her misty veils,
changing her shape.

In the groves of her royal court,
handmaiden sequoias
await her whims.

Below, in the subject valley,
the citizens wake in awe;
enchanted, they drop their coverlets,
postpone their morning coffee
till the mounting Prince burns through.

Now ferries and cars push on
to the lesser summits of the city,
the naked princess abandoned for the day.

The Woman Who Feared Statues

avoided Liberty Dimes
and the bas-reliefs of downtown banks.
She couldn't breathe near porticoes,
panicked at the pedestals,
balked at marble and bronze.

Years back, she had moved to a farm
in Kansas where she stared at the sky,
but even the giant threshers
made her edgy.

In her darkest dreams, she searched
for something on threat of death
through the streets of the Capitol City
where any turn might lead
to a horsebacked general.

Under the quilts of wheatfield nights
she felt herself chilled
by the shadows of obelisks,
impaled on Iwo Jima flagstaffs,
and, as if endlessly tethered,
circling the domed temple
between whose columns Jefferson
leered and hid, shamelessly winking,
hectoring on about
"the pursuit of happiness."

She avoided the angry lions
that guarded the bridge
to the national boneyard,
but found herself caught
between Lincoln's mammoth knees.
Tourists abused her with cameras

whose flashbulbs flared
like an amber Kansas dawn.

In her will
she prescribed an unmarked grave.

Heat Wave

August envelops my skin
tacky as drying lacquer.

The leaves float heavily
laden with insects.

The sun plates
mortar to the trowel,

the clouds no longer
throw shadows,

and the oil leaks of winter
spread and run downhill.

Homage for Luis Tiant

Consider the slow descent of the gloved ball,
the crazy, saw-tooth wriggle
(that dread move to first)
and all those joints that fly out,
your eyes on someone in the bleachers,
the ball, pitched from under the dugout,
nibbling the corners, as they say.

Eight speeds and twelve deliveries—
you are like the poet with many voices.

I've watched you set them up
with the ball that cuts
the distance to the plate
in half and half and half and
only gets there by some miracle.
And then that junk fastball:
everything is relative.

You are art for art's sake on the mound.

Sometimes they hit you, Luis,
bad.
You hang a high one.

This is because
there is no justice.

Luis, you are too happy,
win or lose.

You've got nothing, old man,
but style.

You show us what it is.

The Skyscraper Remembers His Lover's Embrace

She pressed against my penthouse with her cheek,
letting her soft hair tangle
in my roofgarden's sooty shrubs.
I felt her toes work through the sidewalk traps
and down into my basement;
they wiggled past storage pens
and up against the purring boiler.
My ballroom windows caved to her knees.

When she sighed her sigh of passion,
my elevator wobbled in its shaft.
Her belly hove against the fourteenth floor,
and her breasts pushed in my vacancies.
A lover's suite crumbled in her arms.

In this embrace, we nearly slept,
holding each other up.

I was left more hovel than hotel,
ready to collapse into my lobby.

Only later, when she was home alone,
sitting on the corner of her bed,
did she lean over to pull out
the splinters of broken flagstaffs
and flick away the gargoyles
still clinging to her shins.

Crossing the Chesapeake in Winter

From this bridge that arcs
like the spine of a lover's back,
the broad bay seems a black and white
aerial photo of farmland, silver-tipped,
the fences and walls exchanged
for the zig-zag gaps in the heaving ice,
the fields in rhomboid and trapezoid
sheets that subdue the struggling waves.
Oh what a weight this winter has placed
on this frail and fecund sea.

To see it like this,
the bay in its glacial mask,
makes one image the world of mussel and crab
as a place of secret secretions:
crystal, claw, and shell. —And ice
as the skeleton house of salt and blood.

Your tires follow the vanishing arch
raised by fog-kissed buttresses
against which ice-fields nuzzle and split,
and deep in your fingers' flesh
the steering wheel winces
as the bridge cushions the ice
that is traveling somewhere too.

As you reach mid-bay
the channels of open water widen;
the scattering ice-slabs mirror
the bleachy clouds in a darkening sky.
Below, a lone gull captains his raft of ice;
beyond, the horns of distant ships
blast out their names on the frosted air.

In This America: January 1981

In this America
trucks full of hot asphalt
follow the late edge
of morning rush hour,
stitching the cracks of the earth's
heave and sigh.

Junior managers look out
from hothouse Chicago lobbies
wondering only if they should dash
across the glacial space
to the overheated coffeeshops
without struggling in and out of overcoats.

In San Francisco, it's still fall, —
or spring already. Who can tell?
Time is the slow shuttle of work crews
painting the Golden Gate.

People are ready to endure
the hemorrhage of in-depth
reports on the new administration's
first hundred days.

Across much of this land,
one lane of highway is always lost;
one revolving door is jammed shut;
one man with a briefcase
hitchhikes in from Sausalito or Teaneck;
one man is President.

In an Atlanta church,
black faces rise up
like clenched fists.

III

Here at Last

We had come to kiss the living land of memory,
to mingle our laughs and astonished gasps
with the breath of prophets and kings.

In the sun-bleached, rocky hills
we drank the scarce dew of survival;
in the mud of a child-sized Jordan,
we dug our toes, blessing our luck;
in the reaches of blood-brown desert,
our shadows vanished.

Here at last.

Wherever we went, we strode
through the central fact of our lives:
the ancient synagogues of S'fad,
the pinnacle of Herod's Masada
with its buried cries
volleying through our hearts,
the factories and museums
that make the time-line of Israel
a rope for tug-of-war.

By the Tel Aviv shore
we watched the soldiers
sit out front of the bright hotels,
rifles slung over their knees,
inspecting packages and ogling girls.

In the lush orchards of Sharon
our senses bit through the skin and pride
into the flesh and juice of the land.

In Jerusalem, our footsteps
followed the paths of prayer
to the shuddering quiet of joy.

And everywhere,
in every marketplace,
the same faces greeted us,
the same knowing eyes burned back
the question of seeing us
here at last.

Where had we been so long?

Caesaria

Its smooth stones rise
like teeth from a lip of sea,
and this old stone smile
is rinsed by a setting sun
that makes its way to Rome,
like a runner from the far outpost
making his torchlit way
to the emperor's feet.

We wind through the corridors and towers,
we sit on the fallen columns,
we enter the amphitheatre,
expecting a voice.

The fortress walls are tongued
by the sultry bay.

Our own voices are lost winds
in the smooth stones
of our dry mouths.

Caesaria.

Haifa Works (August 1979)

A white charm enameled by the sun,
the city clings to a shoreline chain
encircling the blue neck of sea.

The sailors peer into the shadows,
awaiting the port-town action,
and, bewildered, return to their ships.

"Haifa works," the saying goes,
"Tel Aviv dances, Jerusalem studies and prays."
Sailors will find nothing here, especially today.

The Dan Carmel restaurant is closed
to the public; the flags of three nations
expectantly lick in the wind.

Within, the ministers meet,
performing the slow work of peace
that is beauty: a beauty

unlike the beauty of prayer or play,
but like that of Haifa herself,
the white-washed beauty of work—

tedious, careful,
as intricate as cloisonne.

At the Lebanese Border

We stand near the Good Fence,
mixed with a crowd
of Rhodesian Boyscouts
touring the same outpost.

A young boy in Lebanon
takes down a bucket from his donkey's back
and brings it to the yellow tanker truck
that carries water from the Galilee.

He crosses the same line
that his mother crosses to a clinic
flagged with David's star,
that his brother crosses to a job
somewhere in the hills behind us.

Though the sky is filled
with birds of retaliation,
milk and honey flow out
of one promised land
into another.

Rhodesian Boyscouts lift their cameras
and frame the boy standing between two lands.

And the boy hoists the bucket
onto his donkey.
Then the two of them stir
the dust homeward.

Tonight, in the Christian Arab village,
they will drink from the waters
that Jesus fished.

Bus Number One

When Bus Number One
snakes through Western Jerusalem
to its journey's end at the Wailing Wall,
it is packed tighter than any boxcar
bound for its final stop.

It is filled at the first stop,
yet all along the way,
while not one soul gets off,
crowds clamor to get on.

As it stumbles through Mea She'arim,
blackcoated, bearded men
in broadbrimmed hats
flit magically into the spaceless aisles
like dybbuks, like risen ghosts
of a thousand pogroms.

And as the Dung Gate sneaks into view,
the brilliant morning air
is filled with the squall of lamentation:
the steaming gases of prayer
rise from the lips of the living
and the dead.

False Alarm

It is evening in Jerusalem.
We drive by the floodlit walls
of the Old City
and enter through Jaffa Gate.

We are numb with the lassitude of history,
the dull, small echoes of prayers
at the Wailing Wall,
the mazes of fitted stone,

when the roar of troop-filled trucks
converges before us,
and figures in khaki leap down
slinging machineguns.

My friend leans out of his car,
alert to our fear of the terrorist bomb
that hasn't been sounded.

He chats with the silhouettes
who laugh at his questions.
He turns to me and says,

"Calm down, no trouble tonight.
They have all decided to eat
at the same restaurant.

And don't worry, Philip,
I will protect you. I
am a soldier, too. We are all
soldiers here."

The Price of Survival

When we say we are all soldiers here,
it also means that this highway
is an aircraft runway,
this tourbus a troop-carrier
or an ambulance.

It means that this anchor
is a claw for scaling mountains.

It means that all these plowshares
can be turned to swords
and these pruning hooks to spears.

It means that this leather is armor,
these diamonds are bullets,
and these stacked crates full of oranges
are arsenals of bombs.

And do you know that
at the Technion in Haifa
we have engineered a giant Eucalyptus tree
a grove of which can drain the broadest waters
if by some chance they push us into the sea?

The Dead Sea

You can walk in as gently as a lover,
as carefully as a high-wire dancer,
but you cannot keep from stirring
up salt-clouds whose crystals
will cling to the hair on your legs.

Buoyed by this warm, gravy-like sea,
you are poised like a bright button
stuck in the glue of a child's collage.

As the sun drinks in its endless draught,
the sea shrinks back upon you,
congeals within its socket,
stranding the new hotels
and the mystical shrines for hydrotherapy
inch by rainless inch.

And the small hillocks of salt
rise like snow-mounds
out of a glacier.

Change

Beside the road from Arad to Beersheba
you can see the Bedouin camped.

Their tents are strewn black dice
on the tan, dry lawn of rock.

Huddles of goats and sheep
graze for invisible juices.

It has been this way forever,
the goats and sheep, the roaming figures
in loose-fitting, sun-soaked robes.

But here and there
in the shadow of powerlines
that spark from some dynamo
down through the Negev,
one sees the signs of change:

the antennas of TV sets
piercing the black cloth homes,
the stark contradiction of nomads
tending a farm.

The Red Sea

When you stand by the Red Sea,
you could swear you're seeing
the deepest blue of gems,
the prayerful blue of flooded eyes.

It is a strong blue sea
that gives up the blue-green
stones of Eilat
and breeds a rainbow of fish.

You will hear a dozen stories
of how this warm passage was named:
stories of spilled blood,
stories of glinting evening suns,
reflected red clay hills . . .
or was it first the Reed Sea?

No matter.

King Solomon knew it,
the nearby coppermines red
with their precious lodes, red
with the sweat of empire.

It is this perfect blue
that holds the yellow and peach-toned coral,
that frames the brown silhouette of a lone camel
grazing the Sinai coast.

It is blue with the red of yearning
of those who have crossed the Negev,
their skins gone rusty and dry,
their sun-smitten eyes glowing like coals.

Moshe Jana's Country

In the Tel Aviv home of our Uncle Moshe
you will see potted plants on yesterday's papers
with news of the latest marketplace bombs.

It is like that in Israel.

Come into his small atelier
and look at the work of his brush:
clouds and the sea; on the shore,
full-bodied female figures
comport with bold, handsome stallions.

There are other paintings here too;
these are visions of absence:
his brush has hollowed the space
where the women and horses should be.

And only the spaces that wait to contain them
are real; the rest is a dream.

Or maybe the dreams
and their empty spaces
are all mixed up.

Israel is like that.

The women in Jana's statues
are as firm as the stony ground:
their limbs are heavily-muscled;
their hips and breasts swell
like the hills of Judea;
their eyes look a long way down
over their own landscapes.

His wife loves to dress them up.
Bedecked in Rachel's necklaces,
each wears a droll touch of modesty,
their open nakedness tamed
with a wink of glitter.

Israel is like that, too.

IV

Head, Heart

My head—it is only the rock
I bring to strike against others,
uncovered always, sparking in contact,
or lolling on its stem
like an overgrown seedpod.
It is the ball I roll
toward the pins of light;
it is the hard knot of my senses
and their naive calculations.

My heart, the helmeted one,
floats in the moving shadows,
drives the dark oils that burn
low and steady without flaming,
and is nurtured by them in turn.
It is a tumor, usually benign,
never showing on the x-rays,
known only by its helmet
of bony reasons and white fire.

Too Long

This has gone on too long,
this cool indifference to my miracles.
It smacks of disbelief.
Time was when I'd lose confidence,
depending on your appraisals,
waiting for something in your eyes.
Now I'm telling you
there are changes I can work
whether you see them or not.
I'm telling you once only—
I've had it up to here.

Suppose They Came Unbuttoned

Suppose they came unbuttoned, all your charms,
and tumbled from the harnesses they filled,
and heaped themselves into my waiting arms.

Would you become perplexed and sound alarms,
or would you artfully contrive the way they spilled?
Suppose they came unbuttoned, all your charms,

revealing you a plain of arid farms—
the last grains swiftly harvested and milled
and heaped as loaves into my waiting arms?

And don't think it can't happen. All that swarms
around you now, those drones your radiance has chilled—
suppose they came unbuttoned, all your charms.

Suppose those talismans that kept you from harm's
way flew to me now, the one your glances killed,
and heaped themselves into my waiting arms?

All you have planned so long, the self you've tilled:
the skin, the mind, the heart—all you have willed;
suppose they came unbuttoned, all your charms,
and heaped themselves into my waiting arms.

Walking Away

Let us just walk away from here,
away from the rotation of clothes
in the closet, the question
of eggs or cereal, and the matter
of whether to fill the tank now
or wait until after work.
Let us follow the handiest road
that nobody knows the end of:
the road that never forks
and never comes to a fenced halt.
Let us resist the backward glance,
keep our faces into the wind
though it blows from all directions.
Let us keep our eyes from tearing,
or at least hold the tears
in a heavy film that will not fall.
Let us not remember that we
couldn't have decided anything
if we had considered whether
to take this journey or not,
and let us not pretend that
if we just keep on a bit longer
some destination will present itself.
Hunger will not detain us,
weariness will not alter the pace
with which we pursue this course.
There will be no milestones,
and no seasons will measure
anything at all.
We will not be like birds
or other dumb animals
nor will we be abstruse philosophers.
We will just walk away from here.

We won't worry about shutting the door
or leaving it open
or whether memory distorts
or anything like that.
Our feet will strike out
from this place
and we will just walk.

Definition

As the thumbed mint leaf
snaps back its fresh tang,
I want to snap back, carom,
recoil harder than the felt pressures.

I want to be like new-cut wood
turned sleek under the oiled rag.

I want to bring myself into focus,
to stop this smooth dissolving
into the rest of the world.

I want to throw a sharp shadow
back against its blankness,
step out of the frame
of the liquid mirrors
and dry myself quickly.

Body Language

My knuckles and my bony wrists
show early signs of drying out;
it's harder now to make a fist
for emphasis or rage. This drought
has flaked my skin, and that old spout,
my throat, catches on words it kissed
into the world on its clear liquid days.

Evaporating are the words, thoughts, ways
of doing business in the light.
The night condenses into me, allays
the bonds of my serotinal blight.
Count Dracula and I share in this flight:
we seek moist shadows underneath the quays,
in marrow-darkness bid our bodies twist.

Once You Know How

to track the sun
in its slow arc
you can do it
with your eyes closed
your lids tattooed
by the dull warmth
of dancing vectors
taking you off somewhere
you'll never forget

once you know how
a certain pressure
of the lips can set
your blood on edge
    can do it
with your hands tied
and your fingers
numb with lust
behind your back
wrists throbbing out
of your skin somewhere
you'll never forget.

once you know how
your mind can swallow
whole orchards and oceans
dawdle through instances
that vanish   *you*
can do it in
your sleep   your eyes
tied behind your back
your hands *closed*
lids filled with blood
wrists raised to the sun
you'll never forget

the things you won't forget
—not swimming, making love,
or finding your way home—
you never will have learned
once you know how

Lines on Lines

The man at the edge of the shore
plays out the line with his wrist and eye
to a distance fixed between his worn boots and the sinker.

He has done this thing so often
that the soft whir of the spinning reel
is not even needed to mark the time of the bait's flight.

There is no way to scan it,
no casting of set syllables or figured feet,
but an instinct honed in the hand that gentles the rod

into life.

Turn up your tender palms, friend.
Some claim they can see it there in the lines
that arc and fork and cross just over the map of veins,

but mostly in the life-line:
that hand-held metaphor for all we know
of times and distances that anchor when they must.

It is against that crease
the caster fits the handle of the rod,
along that rod his thumb points toward line's end.

Post-Modern Windows

Look out of this window
one frame of glass at a time.
Through the lower left hand square
see the top of a gas lamp
against some shrubs and half a house.
The upper right panel shows
a chimney under a sweep of sky
skewered by telephone wires.
This is as it should be;
one clear tree deserves another.
The middle panels are filled
by street segments and chunks of cars.
When these pieces are fitted together
the scene is coherent beyond belief.
It's as if someone *knows*
there is one best way
to arrange these squares,
but perhaps this is an illusion
and we are all dupes
of the Grand Glazier.
Try moving the panels around:
a road divided by cirrus clouds,
a car parked on your neighbor's roof.
This is better than canned silence.
Now you raise the ante:
exchange a few squares from this window
with those from others around the house,
or take these with you on vacation
for some splotches of the familiar
to keep your sense of place intact.
Pin one on your sweater.
And, of course, bring back souvenir squares
of ocean, of ski-slope and mountain pine,
to place among the sections
of fenced grasses, tight-lipped garages,
aerobic swingsets, and rusty shoveled places
policed by displaced birds.

Moving Through Ourselves

"We walk through ourselves."
James Joyce, *Ulysses*

We swim through ourselves,
gills pulsing the womb away,
the light condensed to a single cell
charged with the sun's exploding breath.
And back we swim, cutting across the tide,
across our own dim dawns,
fins flickering in starlight.

We crawl through ourselves,
looking for prey. Inside these forests
our claws deepen the old prints,
our fangs grind on the same old roots.
Over and over, we bloody the same kill.
Over and over, we survive.
And we crawl back across the clearing.
Now, camouflaged as meteors, we streak
on the far hunt, our rockets readied.
Ravenous, we whir and click
on the other side of other moons.

We walk through ourselves
and the selves of others;
each step falls in a separate room.
We put our toys away and go to work,
and bring our parents back to the rooms
our children have left.
We swallow the same light and air
that we have before.
And backward and forward we walk:
we walk through ourselves.

Recitation

Today I speak to you for the first time,
a little posing in my voice,
and your listening is frightening.
We don't know each other yet
and you are wondering if this is a man
speaking his poems, the poems speaking,
or the man just being what he is
in things he calls poems.
Though I go on reciting
without answering this question,
I am wondering about it, too.
When I look up from this page
you are already turning away,
or trying too hard to meet my eye.
Some of you—old hands at this—
are offering me closed lids,
pretending this helps you to be attentive.

We are both hoping that something will happen
that changes our lives
the way being yourself for a moment
changes the false inherited pasts
we labor beneath.

These stunts in our jumble of tongues
are my way of preparing to listen,
again, to your various lives.
This is not a one-way conversation,
but a part in the chorus we all comprise.

Between us, unspoken, the words are forming,
rising out of the effort we make
to hear what it is that is waiting to call,
ready to give us our true names
and to set us down at last
in the place we don't dare dream of.

What doesn't happen today
may happen tomorrow,
when I speak to you the next time,
or you speak to me,
both of us listening, listening,
hoping to hear,
leaving a silent space for its coming.
Together we'll hear it, we'll know it,
we'll hear it together, feel it spread through us,
together, we'll say it, we'll speak it,
together, one voice, we will speak it,
for the first time.

Sometimes, Late in the Night

I find, to my surprise
that I'm not sleeping,
that my eyes are wide open,
and that I am following a sound
along the tracks of tube and bone,
a sound that grows richly brittle at crossroads,
and pulls its long load through slow arcs of darkness.

Now is the time the house cracks its knuckles
and the refrigerator whispers out a song.
The noises of my pulsing body
echo and mix with the house,
the chattering trees,
and the rolling boxcars wailing south.

The whistle, the smoke, the square of moonlight,
the invisible ceiling of this hurtling room, . . .
and then the distances of sleep.

And then the honest, morning sounds
of my feet on the floor,
the water splashing in the basin,
the urgent, waking life in which
that train runs silent and unseen.

Near the Fire was designed by Merrill Leffler, cover design by Hilary Martin, and layout by Mark Esterman. Text was composed by Barbara Shaw at The Writer's Center Bookworks, Bethesda, Maryland, in English Times, a typeface based on Stanley Morison's Times Roman.

Philip K. Jason was born in New York City and raised on Long Island and in the Maryland suburbs of Washington, D.C. He received his Bachelor's Degree from the New School for Social Research and graduate degrees from Georgetown University and the University of Maryland. A college teacher since 1966, Jason is now Professor of English at the United States Naval Academy.

Since 1970, Jason's essays, reviews, and poems have appeared in dozens of periodicals. He has edited two books: the *Anais Nin Reader* and *Shaping: New Poems in Traditional Prosodies.* Since 1979, he has served as co-editor of *Poet Lore,* a national quarterly of world poetry. *Thawing Out,* a chapbook collection of his poems, was published in 1979. Of that book, Dave Smith wrote in the *New England Review,* "Philip Jason's strength is that he does not consider that the ordinary must remain ordinary, but imagines that the ordinary very likely conceals the beauty and truth of our lives."

Jason lives in Potomac, Maryland, with his wife, Ruth, and their two teenage children.

Books from Dryad Press

Roger Aplon, *Stiletto*
Roger Aplon, *Travelling by Dawn's Early Light
  at 120 Miles per Hour*
Denis Boyles, *Maxine's Flattery*
Ann Darr, *Cleared for Landing*
Frank Dwyer, *Looking Wayward*
Roland Flint, *Say It*
Marguerite Harris, ed. *A Tumult for John Berryman*
Philip K. Jason, *Near the Fire*
Philip K. Jason, ed. *Shaping: New Poems in Traditional
  Prosodies*
Philip K. Jason, *Thawing Out*
Rod Jellema, *The Eighth Day: New and Selected Poems*
Rod Jellema, *The Lost Faces*
Rodger Kamenetz, *The Missing Jew* (2nd printing)
Barbara Lefcowitz, *The Wild Piano*
Merrill Leffler, *Partly Pandemonium, Partly Love*
Neil Lehrman, *Perdut* (a novel)
John Logan, *Poem in Progress*
Linda Pastan, *Setting the Table* (letterpress and trade)
Harry Rand, *The Beginning of Things* (watercolors by
  Mindy Weisel)
Myra Sklarew, *From the Backyard of the Diaspora* (new
  edition)
Susan Sonde, *Inland is Parenthetical*
Sidney Sulkin, *The Secret Seed* (stories and poems)
Reed Whittemore, *The Feel of Rock: Poems of Three
  Decades*
Irving Wilner, *Poems of the Later Years*
Paul Zimmer, *With Wanda: Town & Country Poems*

Send for descriptive catalog
DRYAD PRESS
15 Sherman Avenue
Takoma Park, Maryland 20912